D1371789

Always listen to your heart.
Orianne Lallemand

For Marjane.
Claire Frossard

A Surprise for
Little Mole

By Orianne Lallemand
Illustrations by Claire Frossard

AUZOU

The forest was slowly coming to life under the warm spring sun when . . .

KNOCK - KNOCK - KNOCK!

Who is knocking on my door? thought Little Mole.

3

Mole opened her door, but no one was there.
She looked to the right, no one.
She looked to the left, no one.

Then she heard . . .

UNH!

UNH!

She looked down at the ground. *What's this funny-looking bundle wrapped up in a blanket?* she wondered.

Mole picked up the bundle and carried it into her house.
Sitting near her warm stove, she gently pulled back the blanket
and found . . .

"Well, hello little Baby . . . Who-zit!"

Baby Who-zit was very hungry.
"Poor little thing, what you need is a
bottle," said Mole.

Mole found a bottle and filled it with warm milk. She cradled Who-zit in her arms while he drank. "You're adorable," whispered Mole when he had finished. "But now, we must find your mama!"

Mole wrapped the baby up in the blanket
and they set out to find his mama.

KNOCK - KNOCK - KNOCK!

"The Rabbit family has lots of children. They might know your mama!" Little Mole said to Baby Who-zit as she knocked on the Rabbits' door . . .

"Hello Ruby. Do you know who this baby's mama is?" Mole asked Mrs. Rabbit.

But Ruby shook her head. "No, I've never seen a baby who looked like this one. He looks a little like a bear."

So Little Mole said good-bye and went next door to the Bears' home.

KNOCK - KNOCK - KNOCK!

"Hello Ben," said Little Mole. "Do you know who this baby's mama is?"

But Mr. Bear shook his head. "What a curious looking baby! He has a black and white coat. Could he be a badger?"

So Little Mole said good-bye and
went next door to the Badgers' home.

KNOCK - KNOCK - KNOCK!

"Hello Babette," said Little Mole. "Do you know who this baby's mama is?"

But Mrs. Badger shook her head. "He isn't one of mine. You should ask Owl. He knows everything about everything."

So Little Mole said good-bye and went to find Mr. Owl, but the baby began to cry.

UNH!   UNH!   UNH!

Mole was so busy rocking Baby Who-zit she didn't notice
someone creeping up behind her until she turned and . . .

... WOLF!

she yelled.

He'd startled Little Mole from the tip of her
nose to the tips of her toes.

"Hello, my dear Little Mole," growled Wolf. "You look
uncomfortable carrying that noisy bundle. Give it to me.
I'll take care of it for you."

"Absolutely NOT!" Little Mole growled back.

Fortunately, Mr. Owl had seen everything!

WOLF ALERT!
WOLF ALERT!
WOLF ALERT!

. . . Owl cried, and the whole forest rushed to his aid.
Outnumbered, Wolf ran away.

Mole told Owl how Baby Who-zit had arrived at her door,
and asked, "Do you know his mama?"

"Hmmm," Owl mused. "There's someone at the zoo who looks like Baby Who-zit. She might be his mama."
So Mole and Baby Who-zit set off to find her.

Little Mole slipped through the zoo gate and walked
slowly down the path, searching for Baby Who-zit's
mama. She stopped in front of a sign. "Look, it's you,
Baby Who-zit! Hello, is anyone here?" she called.
A big panda approached her. "Oh, my baby! My baby
has arrived!"cried Mrs. Panda. "Thank you, Mrs. Stork!
Thank you for delivering my baby!"

"Oh, it was nothing!" Little Mole replied as she hurried away.
Back home at last, Little Mole felt sad.

Her house seemed empty now that Baby Who-zit was gone.
And that's when . . .

KNOCK - KNOCK - KNOCK!

Now, who is that? thought Little Mole as she opened the door.

SURPRISE!

"Happy Birthday, Little Mole!"

Little Mole had been so busy with Baby Who-zit, she'd completely forgotten today was her birthday . . . but her friends had remembered!

Managing Director: Gauthier Auzou
Editorial Director: Laura Levy
Editorial Assistant: Marjorie Demaria
Layout: Mylène Gache, Juliette Breton
Production: Jenny Vallée
Project Management for the English Edition: Ariane Laine-Forrest
English Translation: MaryChris Bradley

ISBN: 9782733867327
© 2019, Auzou Books
All rights reserved.
Printed in China.

Originally published as Une surprise pour Petite taupe,
© 2016, Éditions Auzou
All rights reserved.

www.auzou.com

 Rejoignez-nous sur Facebook et suivez l'actualité des Éditions Auzou.
www.facebook.com/auzoujeunesse